LOST
AND
FOUND
IN
HISTORY

To my family—Dad, Cleo, Chloe, Leo, and Arjun—C.B.

Aboriginal and Torres Strait Islander Peoples are advised
that this book contains the names and images of people who
have passed away.

Thames & Hudson wish to acknowledge that Aboriginal and Torres
Strait Islander people are the first storytellers of Australia and the
traditional custodians of the land. We acknowledge their continuing
culture and pay respect to Elders past, present, and future.

Lost and Found in History © 2025 Thames & Hudson Ltd, London
Text and Illustration © 2025 Clara Booth

Consultancy by John Haywood and Lynette Russell

First published in the United States of America in 2025 by
Thames & Hudson Inc., 500 Fifth Avenue, New York, New York 10110

Library of Congress Control Number 2023939931

ISBN 978-0-500-65350-0

Impression 01

Printed and bound in China by C&C Offset Printing Co. Ltd

MIX
Paper | Supporting
responsible forestry
FSC® C008047

Be the first to know about our new releases,
exclusive content and author events by visiting
thamesandhudson.com
thamesandhudsonusa.com
thamesandhudson.com.au

LOST
AND
FOUND
IN
HISTORY

A search-and-find book
by Clara Booth

CONTENTS

Hi! I'm Maya, and this is my friend, Leo. We're on a search-and-find adventure through history.

Every location we visit is packed with historical details for you to find—can you spot them all?

I'm lost in history! Try to find me in every location.

ANCIENT EGYPT

THEBES, EGYPT, 14 BCE

6

Can you find?

- the queen being carried
- a man with a bird's head
- the three Great Pyramids
- four fans on sticks
- a brown cat with a gold collar
- two hungry crocodiles
- an eye drawn on a column
- a man writing on a scroll

Ancient Egypt is hot and dusty,
but there's lots to see and do. Don't jump
in the Nile River or you'll end up as a crocodile's
dinner. Does Queen Nefertiti really need to be
carried everywhere? And how many naps in
the shade can one cat have in a day?

DISCOVER MORE ABOUT ANCIENT EGYPT

RULING PHARAOHS

Queen Nefertiti rules Egypt with her husband Akhenaten. Ancient Egyptian rulers are called Pharaohs. They don't have carriages, so they are carried over the dusty ground by servants, on a chair called a litter.

ANCIENT ARCHITECTURE

Guess what? The three Great **Pyramids** of Giza have already been around for 1,000 years by the time Nefertiti and Akhenaten are in charge.

> Egypt is hot, but a fan bearer can help keep you cool . . . if you're rich or royal, of course.

> Mm . . . A tasty snack.

> When we die, our owners have us **mummified** so we can join them in the afterlife.

THE NILE RIVER

There is hot desert for miles around, but the Nile provides water for all, including hungry crocodiles.

Every year the Nile floods, making the surrounding land **fertile**—great for farming crops.

FURRY FRIENDS

It is good luck to have a pet cat in ancient Egypt. They hunt pests like rodents and snakes. In return they are treated as well as the Pharaohs. The lucky felines even get to wear precious jewels and gold.

ANCIENT WRITING

Ancient Egyptians are famous for their hieroglyphic writing. Hieroglyphs are symbols that represent objects, people, animals, or sounds. They are carved on tombs and temple walls, and are written on papyrus paper by scribes.

I'm Thoth, the god of writing. I have the head of a long-beaked bird called an ibis.

SUPER SCRIBES

Being a scribe is a very important job. Scribes are the only people in ancient Egypt who learn how to read and write hieroglyphs. A scribe might spend their day recording important events, or writing magic spells.

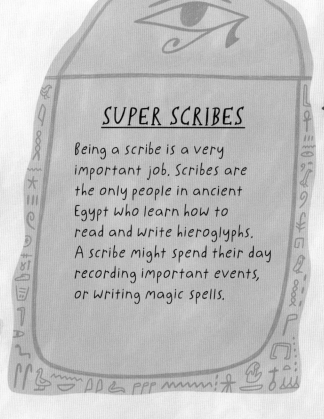

PLANT PAPER

Papyrus paper is made from strips of papyrus plant stems. These are woven together and pressed into a flat sheet. Lots of sheets can be stuck together to make a long scroll.

Did you know that there are over 700 different hieroglyphs? That's a lot to remember!

ANCIENT ROME
ROME, ITALY, 2ND CENTURY CE

When in Rome, the Forum is the place to be. Towering buildings and majestic temples surround the bustling square. The smell of street food fills the air. **Gladiators** prepare for battle at the **Colosseum**. Grab a cup of grape juice— there's so much to explore.

Can you find?

- the emperor in purple
- a big, bronze statue
- a wolf with two babies
- three sacred geese
- a platform covered in spikes
- a gladiator with a net
- a gladiator on a chariot
- a child eating grapes

11

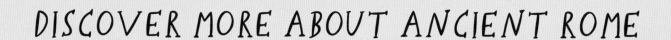

DISCOVER MORE ABOUT ANCIENT ROME

I'm Emperor Hadrian. Do you like my robes? Only emperors get to wear this much purple because it's the most expensive color to make.

A STAGE FOR SPEECHES

The rostra is a big stage where important people, like the emperor, make speeches to the Roman people. It is decorated with spikes taken from enemy warships.

Many Romans don't have kitchens inside their homes, but here at the **tabernae** you can stop for a quick bite.

THE COLOSSUS OF NERO

"Colossal" means "huge" and this bronze statue of Emperor Nero is gigantic—just like Nero's ego. He had the statue built for the entrance to his palace in 68 CE, but Emperor Hadrian had it moved in 128 CE to a new home outside the Colosseum—giving the arena its name.

It took 24 elephants to move me!

LEGENDARY TALES

According to legend, Rome was founded by twin brothers Romulus and Remus, who were raised as babies by a wolf.

Another legend says that Rome was saved from invaders by a flock of **sacred** geese living in a temple. They honked and flapped their wings to warn the guards that the city was under attack.

THE COLOSSEUM

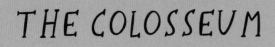

The Colosseum is one of the most famous buildings in Rome. Inside, gladiators fight each other or wild animals to entertain the crowds. There are over twenty different types of gladiator. You can tell the difference by the armor they wear, the weapons they use, and how they fight.

I am a HOPLOMACHUS, which means "armed fighter." I fight using a spear and a short sword.

RETIARIUS gladiators like me carry a net for catching our opponents, and a trident for jabbing them.

You can tell I'm a THRAEX because I have a small shield, a curved sword, and a griffin on my helmet.

We ESSEDARIUS gladiators ride on chariots to escape our opponents and attack them quickly.

Did you know? Gladiator means "swordsman" in Latin.

TANG DYNASTY
CHANG'AN, CHINA, 7TH CENTURY CE

The Chinese city of Chang'an glows under the light of the full moon. The streets are buzzing with activity. In this walled neighborhood—called a ward—there's all sorts of art and entertainment for the people to enjoy, from moonlit poetry to balancing acrobats.

14

Can you find?

- the empress holding a sword
- a basket backpack
- a poet holding a scroll
- two wrestlers wearing ox horns
- three wide-brimmed bamboo hats
- ten red-and-white spotty lanterns
- a ten-layered, red tower
- a woman putting on makeup

DISCOVER MORE ABOUT THE TANG DYNASTY

ROYAL ENTERTAINMENT

At the royal court, Tang rulers impress their guests and show off their power and wealth by throwing huge parties with lots of entertainment.

> The jiaodi wrestling style is a bit like a play where we act like wild oxen. We even wear ox horns when we fight.

> The Tang dynasty is famous for its art and literature. Audiences gather in the streets to listen to stories and poetry.

THE GIANT WILD GOOSE PAGODA

This is one of the most famous buildings from the Tang Dynasty. It was built in around 648 CE with just five stories, but it wasn't very stable and collapsed. 50 years later, Empress Wu had the **pagoda** rebuilt bigger and better with ten stories.

> I am Wu Zetian, the only ancient Chinese empress to rule by myself without a man. Some people say I'm mean, but I think they are just jealous of my success.

> These red paper lanterns symbolize good luck and wealth. They light up festivals and hang outside shops to bring in customers.

DRESSING TO IMPRESS

 WANT TO BE NOTICED IN EMPRESS WU ZETIAN'S CHINA?

Follow her fashion advice for noble ladies.

 Accessorize your hair with jade, pearls, gold pins, and combs.

 Use makeup made from **lead** to make your face pale.

Add a beauty mark on your forehead.

Unsightly pimples? Try a remedy made from bat brains.

Wear a high-waisted skirt, tied with a ribbon.

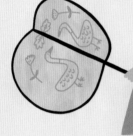

Wear wide sleeves that cover your hands—a sign of politeness when meeting new people.

Farmers like me wear wide-brimmed bamboo hats to protect us from the sun and rain.

As empress, I have lots of outfits for celebrations. This one has a fancy mortarboard hat, upturned silk slippers, and even a ceremonial sword.

EDO KINGDOM
BENIN, NIGERIA, 10TH CENTURY CE

It's a festival day in the great Kingdom of Benin, in West Africa. Giant walls and moats stretch around the city to protect the Edo people and their ruler, the Oba. Try not to get in the way of the sword-throwing chiefs.

Can you find?

- the Oba on his white horse
- two leaf-shaped swords
- three bronze heads in a row
- two hanging fire lamps
- a man making red bead necklaces
- two leopard statues
- a golden bird statue
- a woman holding a white mask

DISCOVER MORE ABOUT THE EDO KINGDOM

THE ALL-POWERFUL OBA

Benin is ruled by the Oba, who makes all the big decisions. It's a tough job with a lot of responsibility, but he has help from his chiefs and advisors.

I am the Iyoba, the Oba's mother. When an Iyoba dies, sculptures of our heads are made to remember us.

This leaf-shaped sword is called an eben. For this special dance, I throw it in the air, but I have to be very careful not to drop it, because it's not allowed to touch the ground.

GREAT GUILDS

Talented craftspeople live and work together in groups called guilds. They share ideas and compete to make the best designs. There are over 40 guilds, including blacksmiths, leather workers, and brass casters.

Look at this beautiful necklace. These coral beads are called ivie. Many Edo people believe that they will protect them from evil spirits and spells.

STREET LAMPS

Benin is one of the first cities in the world to have street lighting. Huge metal lamps fueled by palm oil hang from the walls, helping people see where they're going in the dark.

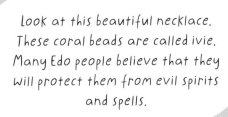

BRONZE CASTING

Benin is famous for its sculptures. Animals, like leopards and birds, represent strength and good fortune, and decorate the Oba's palace. But perhaps the most famous sculptures are the bronze masks.

Making bronze sculptures takes lots of skill. We use the lost-wax casting method. Take a look at how it works.

1. First I make a model out of beeswax and carve details into it.

2. I cover the wax in layers of clay and leave a hole at the top.

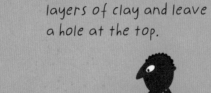

3. I heat the clay over a fire to harden it. The wax inside melts and runs out of the hole. Now I have a clay mold.

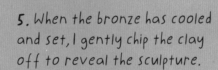

4. I put the clay mold into a pit of hot ashes and pour liquid bronze through the hole to fill the mould.

5. When the bronze has cooled and set, I gently chip the clay off to reveal the sculpture.

6. Finally, I polish the bronze sculpture to make it shiny.

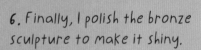

MARVELOUS MASKS

These masks are called Uhunmwu-Ekue. They aren't worn over the face, but are hung from a belt or at the hip.

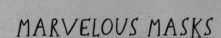

AZTEC CULTURE
VALLEY OF MEXICO, MEXICO, 1519

Aztec Mexico is a vibrant hub of religion and art. Check out these warriors' outfits. The more enemy soldiers they capture, the more decorative the clothing they get to wear. Yikes!

22

Can you find?

- a mother pulling a nose
- a ship with a horse on board
- a girl with a rolling pin
- four ball-game players
- a warrior sipping a chocolate drink
- a white temple, guarded by snakes
- a green mask
- a warrior dressed as a leopard

DISCOVER MORE ABOUT AZTEC CULTURE

WATERY FARMING

There are lots of rivers and lakes in the Valley of Mexico, perfect for growing crops and catching fish. The Aztecs build floating islands called **chinampas** on the water to grow beans, maize (corn), and other vegetables.

> We eat a lot of maize. We grind the kernels into flour to make a dough, then roll it into yummy tortillas.

TASTY CHOCOLATL

This frothy drink is made from cacao beans. Aztecs serve it at **rituals** and festivals, and also use it as medicine. Cacao beans are so valuable that Aztecs use them to pay for things.

> Mm . . . chocolatl.

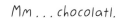

> Our parents believe that pulling and stretching our noses, necks, fingers, and ears will make us bigger and taller. Ouch!

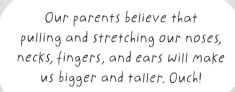

THE CONQUISTADORS

In 1519, ships carrying Spanish soldiers arrive in Mexico. The soldiers—called **conquistadors**—destroy the Aztecs' temples, steal their precious gold, and kill their king. Many people die and their treasures are stolen during this invasion.

AZTEC RITUALS

THE AZTEC CALENDAR

The calendar has two different cycles. The first lasts 365 days and tracks the movement of the sun. The second cycle is just 260 days long and marks different religious ceremonies.

EL TEMPLO MAYOR

Aztec pyramids like this one— El Templo Mayor—are quite different to Egyptian pyramids. They are religious temples where Aztecs pray and make **sacrifices** to their gods, because they believe this will make the sun rise and the crops grow.

These snakes and this mask are decorated with beautiful turquoise stone. The mask represents a fire god, and is worn during ceremonies like the start of a new calendar cycle.

Every 52 years there is a huge festival called the new fire ceremony, which marks when both Aztec calendars begin their cycle on the same day.

This ball game, called Ulama, isn't just for fun. It is also a religious ritual. The game represents a battle between day and night.

25

Look at how busy Tudor London is, not to mention smelly. King Henry VIII sits on the throne, and his second wife, Anne Boleyn, is about to lose her head. Watch out for thieves in your pockets and rats by your feet.

Can you find?

- the king in a gold coat
- the queen in a tower
- a royal trumpeter
- three men playing a board game
- two jousting knights
- a man stuck in the stocks
- three heads on spikes
- ten sneaky rats

DISCOVER MORE ABOUT TUDOR LONDON

CRIME AND PUNISHMENT

Punishment is harsh if you misbehave. Women who gossip have to wear an uncomfortable mask called a scold's bridle. But for the worst crimes—or just making the king angry—you could lose your head.

If you beg or steal you might end up in the **stocks** like me.

How humiliating.

FUN AND GAMES

Wealthy Tudors enjoy sports like **jousting**, where brave knights—and sometimes the king himself—show off their skills.

Jousts are too violent for me! I'd rather exercise my mind with board games like checkers and chess.

JOHN BLANKE

John is one of the king's trumpeters and possibly the most famous Black musician in Tudor London. He performs at important events like **tournaments** and royal weddings.

DISGUSTING DIRT

The streets of Tudor London are filthy. Piles of animal poop and rotting food make it a perfect home for rats and nasty germs. Some people carry bags full of oranges and herbs everywhere. They think the sweet smell will keep the **plague** away.

THE ROYAL COURT

King Henry VIII has around 1,000 **courtiers** and servants living with him. Their jobs range from tasting his wine to wiping his bottom. The king's rich and powerful friends get to enjoy the finer things in life as long as they don't get on his bad side . . . like a few of his poor wives did.

Henry started a brand new Christian religion, the Church of England, just so that he could divorce me and marry Anne Boleyn.

1. CATHERINE OF ARAGON
DIVORCED

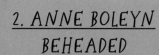

Count yourself lucky. Henry was annoyed that I gave birth to a girl and found an excuse to have me beheaded.

2. ANNE BOLEYN
BEHEADED

I gave Henry the son he always wanted: Edward. But I died soon after he was born.

Well, this is awkward . . .

Henry liked my portrait, but when he met me in person he decided he wasn't into me after all.

3. JANE SEYMOUR
DIED

4. ANNE OF CLEVES
DIVORCED

I was 18 when we married. Henry got jealous that other men liked me and had me beheaded.

Henry was my third husband and I outlived him.

5. CATHERINE HOWARD
BEHEADED

John Blanke once asked Henry for a raise . . . and he got it! That was pretty brave.

6. CATHERINE PARR
SURVIVED

EORA NATION

SYDNEY BASIN, AUSTRALIA, 1788

As the sun sets over the bay, flickering fires light up the evening. Women return to shore with canoes full of fish, and hunters track bouncing kangaroos through the bush. Listen closely, you might hear a kookaburra's laughing song.

Can you find?

- a boomerang
- three spear-wielding hunters
- a lizard on a rock
- five fisherwomen in canoes
- five kangaroos
- ten cooking fires
- carvings inside a cave
- shells on the beach

DISCOVER MORE ABOUT THE EORA NATION

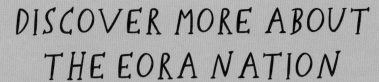

LAND AND LANGUAGE

The Eora nation is made up of different **Indigenous** clans who all speak the same language. Some of the clans include the Gadigal people, the Wangal people, and the Cammeraygal people.

LET'S GO HUNTING

The Eora people hunt animals like wallabies and kangaroos for food. Only the men go hunting, but boys can join in and learn from the adults. Here are some of the tools they use—

Some animals, like cockatoos and goanna lizards are totems—special animals that represent the people and the land. We do not eat them.

The tool on the end of this spear is called a **woomera**. It helps us throw our spears super far through the air.

Boomerangs aren't just for throwing. They can be used for all sorts of things, like digging (to make a firepit or for farming vegetables), hunting, fighting, and even as a musical instrument for dances and ceremonies.

ART AND STORIES

The Eora people are famous for their cave art. Using charcoal, clay, **ocher** pastes, and tools they paint and carve symbols, animals, and images of the Dreamtime—the Indigenous Australian creation story—on cave walls.

FISHING WITH THE FAMILY

While men hunt on land, many Eora women sail into the harbor to fish. They often bring their kids with them, even babies. It's never too early to learn important skills.

My wooden canoe is called a nawi. There is enough space for me, my kids, and even a platform where I can prepare and cook fish on a fire while out on the water.

This strong fishing line is made from the thread of golden orb spiders.

I'm Barangaroo, a fisherwoman and leader from the Cammeraygal clan. When the **colonialists** arrive, I fight to make sure my people's language and culture survives.

STRANGERS FROM BRITAIN

In 1788, British ships land in Australia. The British colonialists do not believe that the land belongs to the Indigenous people. They force many people from their homes and many more are killed. Life in Australia is changed forever.

Did you see a pile of shells on the beach? It's called a midden, and it's made of the shells of mussels, clams, crabs, and other shellfish that people have gathered and eaten.

FRENCH REVOLUTION
PARIS, FRANCE, 1793

The peasants are revolting! In fact, they are having a **revolution**. Unlucky King Louis XVI is about to meet the grim **guillotine**. Statues are pulled down, and fights break out over loaves of bread. It's a dramatic time to say the least, so try not to lose your head!

34

Can you find?

- a flyaway wig
- a loaf of bread
- three ladies knitting
- three garden rakes
- the gruesome guillotine
- ten pointy, red hats
- two men in red-and-white striped pants
- a skirt stuck in a doorway

DU PAIN

DISCOVER MORE ABOUT THE FRENCH REVOLUTION

WHY DID THIS HAPPEN?

French peasants have to pay lots of money to the King and queen, but the rich pay none at all. That's pretty unfair. Bread gets more and more expensive, so the poor are hungry . . . which makes them even more angry.

KING LOUIS

*France has some money problems, but I can't possibly make my wealthy friends pay more **taxes**.*

The commoners will just have to pay extra. What could possibly go wrong?

QUEEN MARIE

TIME FOR A REVOLUTION!

In 1789, the peasants decide that they should be in charge, which means getting rid of the King and Queen, and all their rich friends.

By 1794, both King Louis XVI and queen Marie Antoinette have been beheaded and France is made a **republic**. That means no more kings and queens. Leaders are voted into power by the people.

THE GRUESOME GUILLOTINE

The guillotine is a machine that chops off heads faster than a person with an ax can. Beheadings attract a big audience, including tricoteuses—ladies who do their knitting while they watch.

A little help over here please!

HOW TO SPOT A REVOLUTIONARY

DO'S!
GET THE REVOLUTIONARY LOOK!

RED, WHITE, AND BLUE ARE IN!

KEEP IT SIMPLE!

The Phrygian cap is the accessory to be seen with.

If you can't find a pitchfork, a rake will do the trick.

Breeches and stockings are so last year. It's red-and-white striped pants for the **sans-culottes**.

The tricolor cockade is the hottest symbol of the season (must be worn at all times).

Don't bother with those giant, fussy dresses.

Practical skirt.

GREAT FOR PROTESTING!

DON'TS!
ARISTOCRATS ARE NOT IN FASHION!

AVOID!

WARNING!

Decorative prints are out.

Curly wig.

Ruffled collar.

Breeches really make you stand out as a member of the nobility.

Silk stockings.

VERY EXPENSIVE!

Super tall wigs (look impressive but are often infested with lice).

WAY TOO LUXURIOUS!

Huge panniers (hip pads) easily get stuck in doorways.

NO-NO!

THE ROARING TWENTIES

NEW YORK, U.S.
1926

Can you find?

- a person in a white suit and top hat
- a dancer on a stage
- a piano player
- a bright yellow taxi
- two matching purple dresses
- a golden-roofed skyscraper
- five builders
- two trumpeters

In the city that never sleeps, brand new cars drive through crowded streets. Twinkling skyscrapers tower overhead, and jazz music fills the air. The Roaring Twenties are in full swing.

DISCOVER MORE ABOUT THE ROARING 20S

NEW IN NEW YORK

With a new century comes new inventions that make the world feel bigger and more exciting than ever. For the first time in history, you can hop in a motor car (or yellow taxi cab), drive past towering skyscrapers, and "catch a flick" (20s slang for "movie") at the movie theater. That's "the cat's pajamas" (really cool).

We paint skyscrapers with bright colors and lots of gold—now that's luxurious.

FASHIONABLE FLAPPERS

During World War I, women started doing jobs only men used to do. Now the war is over, women show their independence by dressing fashionably and becoming fabulous *flappers*.

Cloche hat

Long pearl or bead necklace

Bob haircut

Short dress

Straight shape with a low waist

High heels and short dresses are perfect for fast dances.

Heeled shoes

JAZZ MUSIC

The 1920s are sometimes called "the Jazz Age." Jazz is a combination of African American musical styles called "**ragtime**" and "**blues**," with brass band dance music. Meet some famous performers . . .

I'm Bessie Smith, but you can call me "the Empress of Blues," a suitable nickname for one of the most popular Jazz Age singers.

I'm singer Gladys Bentley. I wear a man's white tailcoat and top hat when I perform, which makes me pretty memorable.

I'm Louis Armstrong. My trumpet skills and deep, raspy singing voice are world famous—I even appear in movies.

I'm Duke Ellington. I play piano, sing, lead a jazz band, and compose my own music. It's no wonder I'm invited to perform at the White House.

I'm Josephine Baker. I got super famous performing the fast-paced **Charleston** dance. I become an actress, and even a spy for France during World War II.

Jazz music is played on pianos, guitars, drums, and lots of brass instruments, like the trumpet, trombone, or saxophone.

41

ANSWERS

ANCIENT EGYPT p6-7

- the queen being carried
- a man with a bird's head
- the three Great Pyramids
- four fans on sticks
- a brown cat with a gold collar
- two hungry crocodiles
- an eye drawn on a column
- a man writing on a scroll

ANCIENT ROME p10-11

- the emperor in purple
- a big, bronze statue
- a wolf with two babies
- three sacred geese
- a platform covered in spikes
- a gladiator with a net
- a gladiator on a chariot
- a child eating grapes

TANG DYNASTY p14-15

- three wide-brimmed bamboo hats
- a basket backpack
- a poet holding a scroll
- two wrestlers wearing ox horns
- the empress holding a sword
- ten red-and-white spotty lanterns
- a ten-layered, red tower
- a woman putting on makeup

EDO KINGDOM p18-19

- the Oba on his white horse
- two leaf-shaped swords
- three bronze heads in a row
- two hanging fire lamps
- a man making red bead necklaces
- two leopard statues
- a golden bird statue
- a woman holding a white mask

AZTEC CULTURE p22-23

- a mother pulling a nose
- a ship with a horse on board
- a girl with a rolling pin
- four ball-game players
- a warrior sipping a chocolate drink
- a white temple, guarded by snakes
- a green mask
- a warrior dressed as a leopard

TUDOR LONDON p26-27

- the king in a gold coat
- the queen in a tower
- a royal trumpeter
- three men playing a board game
- two jousting knights
- a man stuck in the stocks
- three heads on spikes
- ten sneaky rats

EORA NATION p30-31

- a boomerang
- three spear-wielding hunters
- a lizard on a rock
- five fisherwomen in canoes
- five kangaroos
- ten cooking fires
- carvings inside a cave
- shells on the beach

FRENCH REVOLUTION p34-35

- a flyaway wig
- a loaf of bread
- three ladies knitting
- three garden rakes
- the gruesome guillotine
- fifteen pointy, red hats
- two men in red-and-white striped pants
- a skirt stuck in a doorway

THE ROARING TWENTIES p38–39

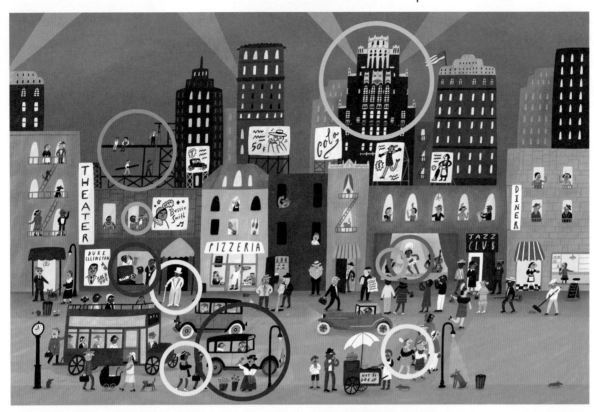

- a person in a white suit and top hat
- a dancer on a stage
- a piano player
- a bright yellow taxi
- two matching purple dresses
- a golden-roofed skyscraper
- five builders
- two trumpeters

What an adventure we've had! Where will you run off to next?

GLOSSARY

Blues—an African American music genre that became popular in the 1920s and 30s.

Boomerangs—curved, wooden tools traditionally used by Indigenous Australian people.

Charleston—a fast dance that became popular in the 1920s.

Chinampas—artificial islands built on lakes by the Aztecs and used to grow crops.

Colosseum—a building in Rome where gladiators fought to entertain the ancient Roman people.

Colonialists—a group of people who start living on land already occupied by another group of people.

Conquistadors—soldiers who sailed from Spain to Mexico and Central America in the 1500s.

Courtier—a person who lives and works in a royal court.

Flapper— a type of woman in the 1920s who dressed fashionably and acted independently.

Fertile (soil or land)—able to produce many plants or crops.

Gladiators—ancient Roman fighters who battled each other or wild animals to entertain audiences.

Indigenous—the native people living in a place, such as the Aztecs in Mexico, or the Eora Nation in Sydney, Australia.

Jousting—a medieval sport where two knights try to knock each other off their horses with long sticks called lances.

Lead—a soft, gray metal used to make face makeup in Tang Dynasty China—though it was poisonous!

Mummified—preserved by removing organs, drying, and wrapping with fabric.

Ocher—a reddish-brown clay that is used to make paints or dyes.

Pagoda—a tower-shaped building with multiple layers, each with a sloped roof.

Plague—a deadly and fast-spreading disease.

Pyramids—buildings with square bases and sloped sides.

Ragtime—a musical style created by African American musicians in the late 1800s.

Revolution—when a country's ruling system or government is overthrown.

Republic—a country where the people choose their leaders by voting for them.

Ritual—ceremonies, usually religious, performed for a specific occasion.

Sacred—something that is important for religious or spiritual reasons.

Sacrifice—something precious that is offered to a god or gods in return for something, such as a good harvest or weather.

Sans-culottes—French for "without breeches," a term used to describe the French revolutionaries.

Stocks—boards that force a person to stand or sit in one place, usually in public, as punishment for a crime.

Tabernae—ancient Roman "fast food" restaurants.

Taxes—money paid by a country's people to the rulers or government.

Tournaments—contests where knights participated in events such as sword duels and jousting.

ABOUT THE AUTHOR

Clara Booth is an illustrator based in London.
She graduated with a BA from Camberwell
College of Art in 2022 and has illustrated eight
phonics books for early readers. She has also
worked for Kew and the BFI. This is her first
book as an author-illustrator.